Peanut Picking

by Patricia M. Stockland
illustrated by Ryan Haugen

visit us at
www.abdopublishing.com

Published by Magic Wagon, a division of the ABDO Publishing Group, 8000 West 78th Street, Edina, Minnesota, 55439. Copyright © 2008 by Abdo Consulting Group, Inc. International copyrights reserved in all countries. All rights reserved. No part of this book may be reproduced in any form without written permission from the publisher.
Looking Glass Library™ is a trademark and logo of Magic Wagon.

Printed in the United States.

Text by Patricia M. Stockland
Illustrations by Ryan Haugen
Edited by Nadia Higgins
Interior layout and design by Becky Daum
Cover design by Becky Daum

Library of Congress Cataloging-in-Publication Data
Stockland, Patricia M.
  Peanut picking / Patricia M. Stockland ; illustrated by Ryan Haugen.
    p. cm. — (Safari friends—Milo & Eddie)
  ISBN 978-1-60270-085-7
 [1. Monkeys—Fiction. 2. Elephants—Fiction. 3. Individuality—Fiction. 4. Friendship—Fiction. 5. Grasslands—Fiction. 6. Africa—Fiction.] I. Haugen, Ryan, 1972- ill. II. Title.
PZ7.S865Pea 2008
[E]—dc22
                                                        2007036990

Deep in the heart of the great, great grasslands, Milo the monkey sat scratching his head. He was lost. Home was neither close nor far, and although he wasn't afraid, the ground had just begun to rumble.

"That's odd," Milo thought. "The trees never shake in the jungle."

RUMBLE! RUMBLE! RUMBLE!

Milo waited to see what would happen. Then he saw clouds of dust blowing above a stand of trees.

"Hmmmmmm," the monkey said. He went to get a better look.

Stomp. Stomp. Stomp. Some elephants were walking in circles. Walking in circles helped the elephants think, and today they had an important problem to solve.

One of the herd was missing again. It was Eddie, because it was always Eddie. Everyone knew that *something* had to be done about *Eddie!*

"I think we should forget him forever," snorted Ella. Ella had a red polka-dot ribbon tied around the end of her trunk. "He's always missing. He can't stay in line. And his trunk doesn't work!" she shouted.

"But if we leave him behind," said Eloise, the oldest elephant, "we won't have enough elephants for peanut picking."

"Duh!" Ella said, smacking her trunk against Eloise's forehead. "His trunk doesn't work, so he *can't* pick peanuts."

The other elephants stared at Eloise. Eloise stared back. She hadn't thought of that. But she did like Eddie, despite his strange, not-so-useful trunk. It didn't seem right to leave him—especially with the great Summer Peanut Party only one week away.

The elephants were still staring. As the oldest elephant, Eloise had to make a decision.

"Alright," she sighed. "We keep moving—we have to be mindful of the party." And with a *humpf* and a great stomping of dust, the elephants were gone.

Milo watched the elephants walk away. "How do you misplace an elephant?" he wondered. Milo decided to find Eddie. It couldn't be that hard to find an elephant— and perhaps there would be a reward of peanuts.

Boom. Boomedy-boom boom. Before Milo even had a chance to stand up, the ground began rumbling again. Milo scooted toward a nearby termite mound just in time to miss being stepped on by none other than Eddie himself.

"Well, hello there!" bellowed Eddie at the bewildered monkey. "I don't suppose you've seen a herd of elephants around here?"

"Why, yes, I have," Milo replied. "Are you Eddie?"

"Absolutely, I am Eddie! How did you know?"

"Just a guess," Milo said. "I think the other elephants have gone on without you."

"Is that a fact?" asked Eddie. "I'm helping find peanuts for the Summer Peanut Party. I wonder why they would leave without me."

"Well," Milo said, "I hate to spread gossip, but I heard them mention something about your trunk not exactly, um, being up to snuff."

"Oh." At that, Eddie's floppy ears and trunk and every wrinkly wrinkle on his body seemed to droop.

It was true, after all. His trunk didn't work. The other elephants never said anything about it to Eddie's face, but he knew they noticed. When it was time to trumpet, spray water, move branches, or pick peanuts, they always stared at Eddie.

"I have to get going," Eddie said to Milo, slowly turning around.

"Where are you going?" Milo asked.

"Who knows? Who cares?" Eddie said, looking more droopy than ever.

"Wait! I can help you!" Milo shouted. "I think I know where they went. And who cares if your trunk doesn't work? There must be something else about you that's special. We'll show them!"

Eddie wasn't exactly convinced, but Milo seemed nice and neither of them was very busy at the moment.

"Well, okay," Eddie said. And off went the monkey and the elephant through the great, great grasslands toward the peanut patch.

Meanwhile, the other elephants were just arriving at this special place. The elephants came to the peanut patch once a year to pick peanuts for the Summer Peanut Party. This had been a tradition since before any animal in the grassland could remember—even the elephants.

This year they noticed something new at the peanut patch. There was a sign with some marks on it.

"Huh?" Eloise said, walking up to it. "Does anybody know what this sign says?"

The elephants shook their heads. Elephants are pretty smart, but none of them could read. So, they entered the patch and proceeded to pick.

Just then, Milo and Eddie walked up to the patch. They were still trying to think of special things about Eddie.

"Can you juggle?" Milo asked.

"No," said Eddie.

"Tell the future?"

"No."

"Tap dance? Do a somersault? Knit a scarf?"

But the answer was always no, no, no.

When Eddie saw the other elephants inside the patch, he said to Milo, "Well, here we are with nothing special to report. What *now?*"

The other elephants noticed Eddie, but they just rolled their eyes and went back to work.

Eddie and Milo stood in place for a minute. They wondered what to do. Then they noticed the sign. Eddie read aloud:

"PLEASE DON'T PICK THE PEANUTS.

THEY'RE POISONOUS!

APPLY WATER TO ANYONE WHO'S PICKED THESE POISONOUS PEANUTS."

"What!?" shouted Eddie.

"What!?" shouted Milo.

"The peanuts!" yelled Eddie. "I have to stop the picking!"

"Eureka! That's it!" yelled Milo. "That's your something special! You can read!"

Eddie didn't hear Milo. He had already dashed into the peanut patch. "Eloise! Ella! Everyone! Stop picking! The peanuts are poisonous!"

Just then, the elephants started to shake and quake. Some of them even rolled on the ground.

"Water! Water!" Eddie shouted. He ran to the hydrant, stomped on the hose, and began spraying the herd.

Within minutes, the elephants were soaked. The peanut dust had washed away, along with all of the peanuts, but the elephants were saved.

"Is everyone OK?" Eddie asked. "I'm sorry about the mess, but the peanuts are poisonous."

"How did you know?" asked Ella, still shaking off water.

"He can *read!*" Milo shouted. "He read it on the sign!"

Everyone stared at the monkey. Then they stared at Eddie. Eddie just shrugged.

"Why didn't you tell us?" asked Eloise.

"I thought it was just another thing that made me weird," answered Eddie. "Like when my trunk doesn't work and I can't stay in line and I keep getting lost."

"Well," Ella answered, "maybe those things aren't bad after all. Let's get out of here and find another peanut patch."

"I think I know where one is," answered Eddie. "I found it once when I was lost!"

And with that, Eddie, Ella, Eloise, the other elephants, and Milo set off across the great, great grasslands. This time, no one felt lost.

Savanna Facts

African elephants eat a variety of foods, including grasses, tree bark, leaves, herbs, and fruits.

An African elephant in the savanna lives, on average, for 60 years.

Elephants can use their trunks for a number of things, including handling small objects, tearing down large branches, and breathing (like a snorkel) underwater!